The Gift of Herbert Grunch

By
G. B. Austin

For
Baily
Brandon
Elijah
Elienai
Ezekiel
and Journey

My Kids
My inspiration

And thank you Michelle,

My bride,

...without whose love and
support this book would not have been made.

Most people like Christmas a bunch,
and, truth is, so did Herbert Grunch.
He liked the food, the games, the smells,
the way children played with their toys...

The red ribbons, the silver bells...
He didn't even mind the noise.

But one thing Herbert Grunch Liked most
at Christmas time was to host.

Every year Herbert would write a list of people he'd invite.

Uncle Gene who fixed his furnace, his mom who sold appliances, Aunt Nadine the taxidermist, his cousin Tom who built fences.

With all the people he'd invite
To join in holiday fun,
He had to make his house just right
to show he was a good person.

So Herbert Grunch would scrub and scrub
the counters, floors, and the bathtub...
Shine the windows, wax the ceiling,
sweep and mop the basement stairs.
Make sure the housepaint wasn't peeling,
get out the celebration chairs.

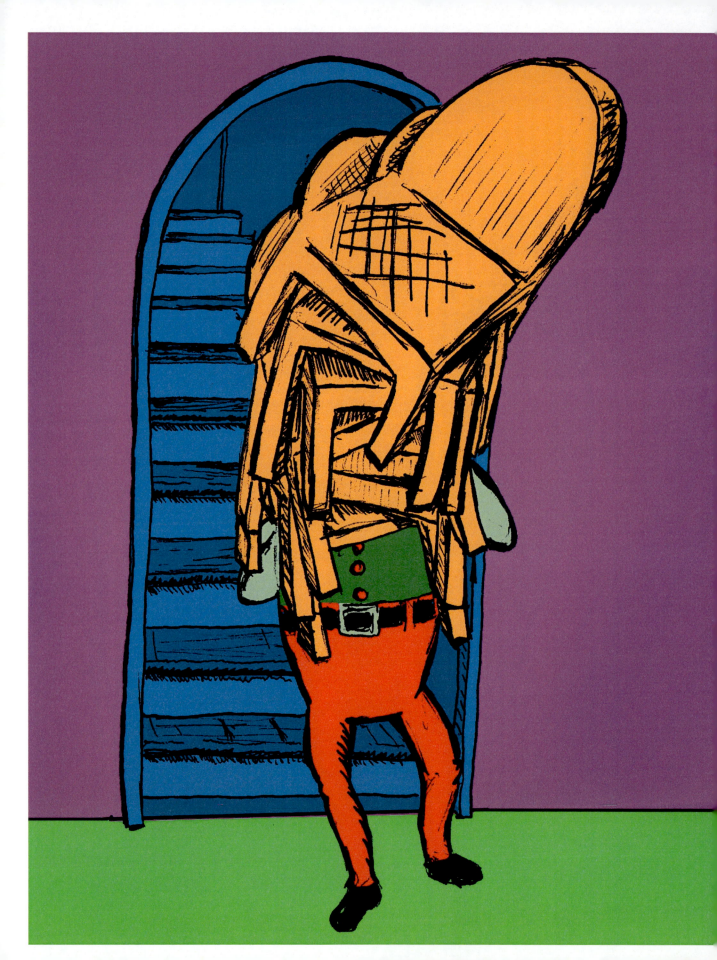

"Since cleanliness is godliness"
He thought the Bible said somewhere,

"But God made dirt,
and dirt's a mess.

But dirt don't hurt...

Well, I don't care-
I'll swiffle this,
and hoovle that,
and slurk up ev'ry
dinner splat."

He fantasized that on the night
when Christ was born outside the inn,
had Grunch been there he'd make it right,
and make the newborn savior grin!

The shepherd's beards would all be combed,
their feet wiped off, the place kept so
the angels would feel so at home,
they would give him his own halo.

He cleaned,

... And cleaned until
there was only one thing to do...
a chore that Herbert Grunch abhored
which I think makes him much like you...

For if there were one thing he'd wish,
one fate, one goal in all his life,
it'd be never to wash a dish,
or plate, or bowl, or even knife...

He said, "I will not clean this pan. I do not like to clean by hand.
I will not clean this dish or cup. There must be something I'll think up."

He stood upon a kitchen tile, looking intently at the sink,
and just stood there for a long while, till he could not ignore the stink.

Then Grunch said out loud to no one,
"It's time that I did what makes sense
about this job that must be done,
I'll buy a brand new appliance!"

So he picked out a new machine
and installed it by himself
to grab a dish
and wash it clean
and dry and stack
it on the shelf.

The house was clean, the job was done.
But all his thoughts were a muddle.
For though his new
machine did run,
he was standing
in a puddle.

So here we find him
on the phone,
two times transfered
and twice on hold,
waiting, waiting,
to gripe and moan,
and let his story unfold.

A man picked up and said "Hello.
and thanks for holding, my name's Joe"

"Yes Joe, I finally got through.
Could you help me with my loose screw?
You see, it holds open the door,
and now the leak is on the floor."

"Mr. Grunch sir, question one now,
'would you say it doesn't run now?'"

"It washes bowls, it washes cups-
but I think he who tightens ups
the screw was on a coffee break,
and yet they sent it by mistake!"

"And now the leak is on the floor!
And when the floor began to warp
it caused my grandpa clock to tip,
which capsized my model ship!"

"It sunk your ship now? You don't say?"
You are in the wrong branch my friend.
You need Nautical Means and Ways."
  Then he put him on hold again.

Meanwhile, his cotton rug had shrunk
and pulled the legs out from the chair,
Which tipped and knocked down his stuffed skunk,
and his Jar of Elvis hair.

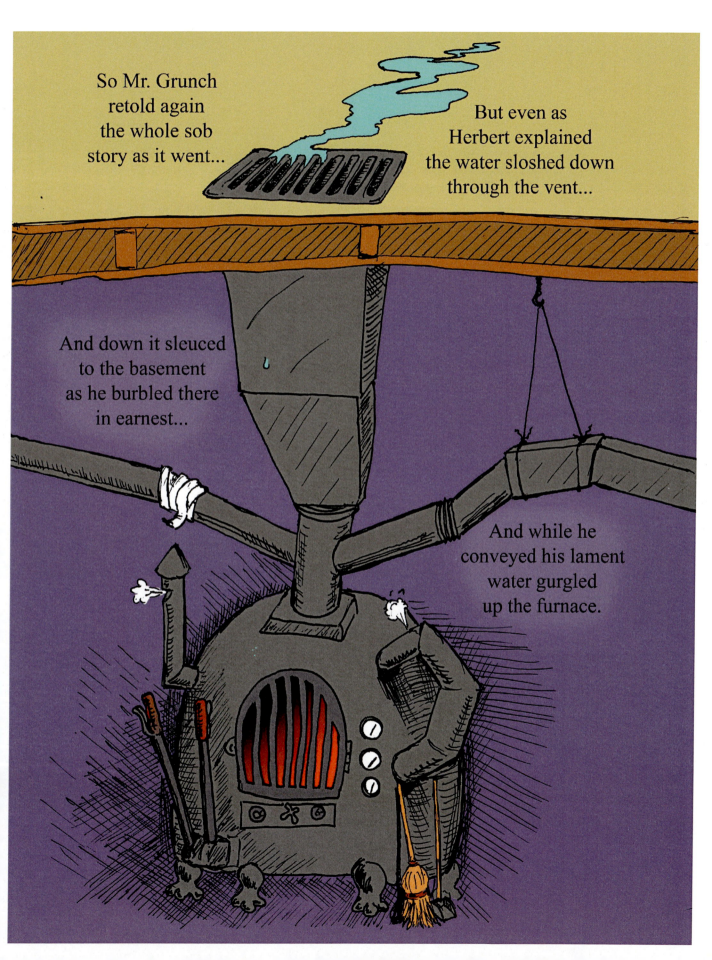

"So Mr. Grunch, what would you like?
Perhapse some rainbow trout or pike?
we have tropical fish too.
They come in colors
red and blue.
I can see your
problem's dire, so,
we'll appease you with these fishes."

"About the fish I can't say no,
but how will I wash my dishes?"

Since Nautical Means
didn't know,
they transfered him
right back to Joe.

"Sir Grunch, it's time
for question 2.
'Why didn't you
tighten that screw?'"

"Because I did not
screw that screw!
That screw was
not my job to do!
They told me this
dishwasher's 'The bomb.'
I even bought it from my Mom!
I ordered it and brought it home,
broke down the box, threw out the foam.
The directions told me what to do,
and never mentioned that door screw!
I always try to do my best
to clean my house for all my guests,
but your dishwasher has transgressed
and swamped my house, and made a mess!"

Then off his shelf

a Christmas elf

a trinket he made

by himself,

began to fall

beside the wall.....

And bounced off of a rubber ball.
And just before it hit the floor...

...That rolled downstairs and down the hall...

And though he dove to try and stop it...

Right through the door the ball had crashed...

... His fence was smashed!
and when the Grunch's gate came down,
his great oak lattice came down next
which beat upun the muddy ground,
knocking the legs out from his decks!

"Could you answer question four now?"

"No! The guests are at the door now!
And here, I have nothing to give,
no place to host, nowhere to live-
except the barn, which is intact.
But all the niceties it lacks!"

"I need to take a breath of air."
He sat down in his rocking chair,
but since the water spread so fast,
he slipped and fell down on his back side.

But when a knock came at the door
he picked himself up off the floor.

"Time to put this party in gear."
Herbert Grunch moaned under his breath.

He snatched some tinsel and holley,
and some red and green Christmas socks.

And in his barn he gathered all
the loved ones he'd invited.
He wore a smile and stood up tall
and tried to seem excited.

But as the night wore on he found
the crowd of mirthers dwindling.
The ones he thought would stick around
were splitting much like kindling.

His cousins Ned, Fred, Ed, and Gene
had faded out one at a time.
His uncle Ted and aunt Nadine
didn't even stay for the mime.
And like a kick when he was down,
he saw grandma Grape defected.
So here we find him with a frown,
feeling a little dejected.

Then... little Leanne Liylah Lay
whose fourth Christmas Eve was today,
noticed that he looked this way
and left the candied yams she had.

She walked right up to him to say...

"Oh Grunchy, why do you look so sad?
Your face looks kind of pale and scrunchy.
Did you get older uncle Grunchy?"

"Oh sweety, I'm just sad to see
that people were not having fun.
So many of my family
have left before
the party's done.
The barn smells like
damp socks and pork,
the food is cold
and it's boring…

...Some of the upstairs lights don't work. I can hear old Earl is snoring.
I worked so hard all on my own so all of you could enjoy it.
It's like nothing I did has shown- like some enemy destroyed it.
My deck is nothing but wood beams, I fell out of my rocking chair,
a screw is loose on my machine.-"

"Oh, poor old Grunchy, we don't care.
We all knew you had a screw loose, and that you are short of a full deck.
My Mommy went in to cook your goose and Daddy is an 'arctic-teck.'
He went in to fix your socket so it's not such a shocker."

She put her hand into her pocket.

"They heard you went off your rocker.
So they all went in to make repairs.
You're a great entertainer.
with the lights not all on upstairs,
it's like Jesus in the manger."

Then Herbert thought how on that night
of the holy nativity,
when gifts of gold and myrh and spice
were brought by the wise three,
three others looked down on our mess
from heaven's lofty door.
In perfect, righteous, holiness-
he wasn't fit to mop their floor...

And out of that most holy place
a father sent his only son,
through lightyears of rich outerspace
into a war torn nation.
And through a little teenaged girl,
ostracized from her family,
into our dirty, messy world,
in a tiny fragile body,
he came.
Not to be entertained,
nor for excellent room service,
but to take all our guilt and shame,
and ultimately die for us.

"So Gene went in to fix your furnace, your skunk got fixed by aunt Nadine, and Fred and Phil went with Earnest to fix your 'lettuce,' or something."

Soon Herberts home again looked clean,
almost all of it was set right.
And Grunch could see it wasn't he
who hosted the party that night.

This Christmas eve was to them
like the first Christmas in essence.
Each one brought their gifts to him,
and Jesus came with his presence.

You know, you could have gold to spare,
and fashion, grace and charm...
He doesn't care what clothes you wear,
because he was born in a barn...
and all the riches out in space,
and every treasure ever worn
were His before he graced this place,
long before your grandma was born.

Even if your house is a mess-
though you want to clean it for Him,
your shiny windows won't impress,
your polished floors may bore Him.

But offer Him a heart broken,
and lift up a contright spirit...
Though accusations be spoken
you can know He'll never hear it.

He calls orphans His own children
and takes the messiest of mess,
and turns all our guilt and sin
into clean, perfect, holy, righteousness.